George
the Knight

by Leon Read

Illustrated by Clare Elsom

Crabtree Publishing Company

www.crabtreebooks.com

Crabtree Publishing Company

www.crabtreebooks.com
1-800-387-7650

616 Welland Ave.
St. Catharines, ON
L2M 5V6

PMB 59051, 350 Fifth Ave.
59th Floor,
New York, NY

Published by Crabtree Publishing in 2011

Series Editor: Jackie Hamley
Editor: Reagan Miller
Series Advisors: Dr. Hilary Minns, Catherine Glavina
Series Designer: Peter Scoulding
Project Coordinator: Kathy Middleton

Text © Leon Read 2010
Illustration © Clare Elsom 2010

Printed in Hong Kong/042011/BK20110304

First published in 2010
by Franklin Watts
(A division of Hachette
Children's Books)

The rights of the author and the
illustrator of this Work have
been asserted.

Library and Archives Canada
Cataloguing in Publication

Read, Leon
  George the knight / by Leon Read ; illustrated by
Clare Elsom.

(Tadpoles)
ISBN 978-0-7787-0589-5 (pbk.).--
ISBN 978-0-7787-0578-9 (bound)

  I. Elsom, Clare II. Title. III. Series: Tadpoles
(St. Catharines, Ont.)

PZ7.R233Ge 2011   j823'.92   C2011-900153-5

Library of Congress
Cataloging-in-Publication Data

Read, Leon.
  George the knight / by Leon Read ; illustrated by
Clare Elsom.
      p. cm. -- (Tadpoles)
  Summary: George wants to be a knight, but first he
needs a sword, a shield, and a horse.
  ISBN 978-0-7787-0589-5 (pbk. : alk. paper) --
ISBN 978-0-7787-0578-9 (reinforced library binding :
alk. paper)
  [1. Knights and knighthood--Fiction.] I. Elsom, Clare,
ill. II. Title. III. Series.

  PZ7.R23514Geo 2011
  [E]--dc22

                              2010052363

Here is a list of the words in this story.
Common words:

a	now
are	you
is	your
not	

Other words:

George	knight	where
has	shield	wow
horse	sword	

George is a knight.

"You are not a knight.
Where is your sword?"

4

Now George has
a sword.

"You are not a knight. Where is your shield?"

10

13

Now George has a shield.

"You are not a knight. Where is your horse?"

18

19

"Wow, George!
Now you are a knight."

Puzzle Time

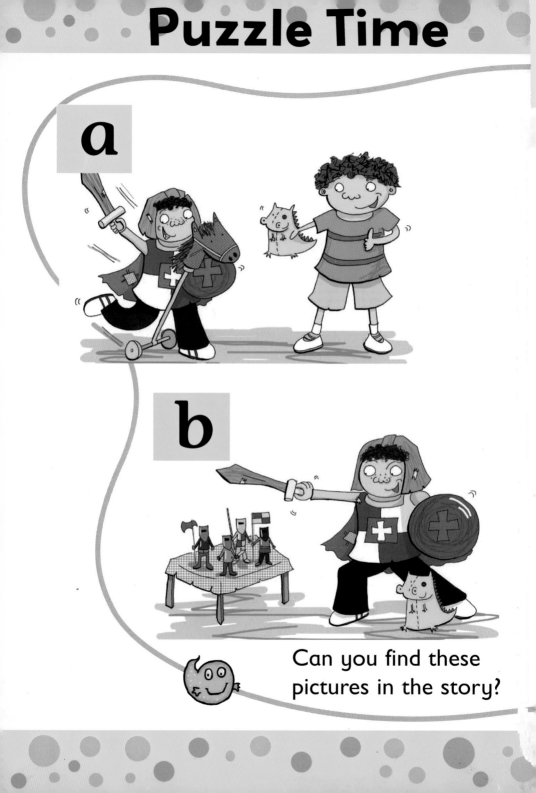

a

b

Can you find these pictures in the story?

Which pages are
the pictures from?

Turn over for the answers!

Answers

The pictures come from these pages:
a. pages 20 and 21
b. pages 14 and 15
c. pages 6 and 7
d. pages 16 and 17

Notes for adults

Tadpoles are structured to provide support for early readers. The stories may also be used by adults for sharing with young children.

Starting to read alone can be daunting. **Tadpoles** help by listing the words in the book for a preview before reading. **Tadpoles** also provide strong visual support and repeat words and phrases. These books will both develop confidence and encourage reading and rereading for pleasure.

If you are reading this book with a child, here are a few suggestions:

1. Make reading fun! Choose a time to read when you and the child are relaxed and have time to share the story.

2. Look at the picture on the front cover and read the blurb on the back cover. What might the story be about? Why might the child like it?

3. Look at the list of words on page two. Can the child identify most of the words?

4. Encourage the child to retell the story using the jumbled picture puzzle on pages 22-23.

5. Discuss the story and see if the child can relate it to his or her own experiences, or perhaps compare it to another story he or she knows.

6. Give praise! Children learn best in a positive environment.

If you enjoyed this book, why not try another **TADPOLES** story?
Please see the back cover for more **TADPOLES** titles.
Visit **www.crabtreebooks.com** for other **Crabtree** books.